THE IMPOSSIBLE PARENTS GO GREEN

Poor Ben and Mary Norm. Their parents have decided to become ecologists and are getting it impossibly wrong. They've got to be stopped ... and quick!

Brian Patten is one of Britain's best-known poets. He has written many volumes of adult poetry while, for children, he has written the popular verse collections *Gargling with Jelly* and *Thawing Frozen Frogs*. Among his other works for children are the award-winning novel *Mr Moon's Last Case*, the Walker picture book *The Magic Bicycle* and the prequel to *The Impossible Parents Go Green*, *Impossible Parents*.

Books by the same author

The Magic Bicycle

Impossible Parents

BRIAN PATTEN

Illustrated by Arthur Robins

WALKER BOOKS
AND SUBSIDIARIES
LONDON · BOSTON · SYDNEY

2005

First published 2000 by
Walker Books Ltd, 87 Vauxhall Walk
London SE11 5HJ

This edition published 2001

2 4 6 8 10 9 7 5 3

Text © 2000 Brian Patten
Illustrations © 2000, 2001 Arthur Robins

This book has been typeset in Garamond

Printed in Great Britain by
St Edmundsbury Press, Bury St Edmunds

British Library Cataloguing in Publication Data:
a catalogue record for this book is
available from the British Library

ISBN 0-7445-7881-7

CONTENTS

CHAPTER ONE

This is Ben and Mary Norm in the classroom.

This is their teacher, Miss Jones.
Miss Jones was an ecologist. She
worried about saving the earth. She
worried about animals and plants
being poisoned and about whales
having their blow-holes bunged up
with babies' dummies. Worrying
about the earth was Miss Jones's
hobby. You can tell how much Miss
Jones worried just by looking at her.

Ben and Mary liked Miss Jones. In the school holidays, they used to see her shovelling dead hedgehogs off busy roads with her poop-scoop. Ben and Mary knew *exactly* who the culprits were – their impossible parents!

One day, Miss Jones decided to teach the class about ecology. She held up a picture of a sweet little fox.

"Can you imagine who would wear a coat made out of this lovely creature?" she asked.

Ben and Mary could... Their mum.

Next, she held up a picture of a canal filled with rubbish.

"Can you imagine what terrible kind of person would do this?" she asked.

Ben and Mary knew very well… Their dad.

For ages after the lesson, Ben and Mary tried to get their parents to change their ways, but Mr and Mrs Norm just carried on doing what they liked doing.

Mrs Norm practised her belly-dancing in front of the mirror.

Mr Norm practised being a pop star with his imaginary guitar.

"It'd be easier talking to a squashed hedgehog than to them," said Mary.

"A squashed hedgehog would have more brains," said Ben.

CHAPTER TWO

Then, one afternoon when Mary
and Ben came home from school,
something very unexpected
happened.

"We're turning Green," said Mrs
Norm.

"Not physically," said Mr Norm. "That would be horrible. What we mean is we're going to become eco … eco … er…"

"Ecologists?" suggested Ben.

"That's it!" said Mr Norm, who was very bad at pronouncing big words. "We're going to follow Miss Jones's example and do our bit to save the earth."

This pleased Ben and Mary, but they were also worried. Their parents were impossible parents.

Ben and Mary thought something was bound to go wrong. And of course, it did.

When Ben and Mary came down for breakfast the next morning, their parents were sitting at the table utterly naked.

"Think of all those poor freezing sheep that have the wool stolen off their backs, just so we can keep warm," said Dad.

"Naked parents are totally vomit-making," said Ben.

"And they wobble," said Mary. "Naked wobbly parents are the most disgusting of all."

"Well, it *is* a bit chilly," decided Mrs Norm, and she sent Dad down to the cellar to find some old potato sacks. She cut out holes for their heads and arms and they wriggled into them.

"You're not driving us to school dressed like that," said Ben.

"Drive? We can't possibly drive you to school," said Mrs Norm.

"No, we're getting rid of the car," said Dad.

"We remembered what you told us about cars polluting the atmosphere with notorious grasses."

"We said obnoxious gasses!" cried Ben, marching out of the house.

Ben and Mary got another surprise at lunchtime.

This is what was inside their lunch boxes:

Yak cheese

Mysterious bits

Bean sprouts

They dumped the lot. Not even the pigeons would eat the stuff.

Then after school they found that
Mum and Dad had thrown out the
telly.

"TV transmissions fry birds' brains,"
said Dad. "Their brains fall out of
their ears and are eaten by worms."

Ben decided Dad's brains had
fallen out of his ears years ago.

Not only did they miss their favourite soap on TV, but when dinner came it was as bad as the stuff in their lunch boxes. They couldn't even *guess* what it was.

Things were no better at bedtime.

First, Dad insisted on candlelight. He said it took the equivalent of an entire forest just to keep an electric light bulb going for an hour. Ben said not even Miss Jones believed *that*.

Then they found
that their duvets
had vanished and
been replaced by
two itchy straw
blankets.

"Duvets are not
ecological," said
Mrs Norm. "They're
stuffed with feathers
plucked from harmless ducks.
A naked duck is a heart-rending
sight," she said.

"But you two haven't seen any
kind of duck for years," said Mary.

"Except those you've cooked,"
said Ben.

Mary and Ben wished they hadn't said anything about ecology to their impossible parents. They decided they had to get them back to their normal impossible selves before things got *really* bad. They needed a fantastic plan. The trouble was, they couldn't think of one.

CHAPTER THREE

At school, Ben and Mary were
having a rotten time. Word had got
round that Mr and Mrs Norm were
wandering the streets wearing
nothing but sacks.

And Mary's worst enemy, Alice Frimp, told everyone that she'd seen Mrs Norm collecting worms from the front garden.

Mary said it wasn't true. But of course no one believed her.

Everyone was much more interested in the idea of Mrs Norm collecting worms for supper.

Mary hated Alice Frimp. She hated her even more than she hated worms. She wished she could change Alice Frimp into a worm.

Mr Norm was also causing
embarrassment. A rumour had got
round that he'd gone into Mr
Azteck's shop to buy some tape to
mend the hole in the ozone layer.

Ben and Mary blushed furiously every time someone mentioned something that their parents had been up to. Not that you could see them blush. They'd developed pimply red rashes from sleeping under the itchy blankets.

CHAPTER FOUR

As the days passed, things got worse. The cat had moved next door because Mum was feeding it vegetarian sausages.

Ben and Mary had started to
wear pegs on their noses because
their parents were eating so many
soya beans that they couldn't stop
passing wind. They sounded like a
pair of old trumpets.

By now, Mary and Ben were only pretending to eat at home. They scraped the food Mum served them into plastic bags and chucked it in the dustbin when no one was looking.

Then they went to their friend Pattie Rotti's house and had secret hamburgers and chips and all the other wonderful stuff Mrs Norm had stopped cooking.

It was at Pattie Rotti's house that a brilliant idea popped into Mary's head. It was the perfect plan for getting their parents back to normal.

When she told Ben the plan, he also thought it was a fantastic idea.

They went to get the stuff they needed to put Mary's plan into action.

First, they went
to the health food
store and bought
a gigantic carton of
Old Yak Yogurt.
Then they mixed
some crunchy
gravel from Pattie Rotti's garden
into it. Then they added a little bit
of cat litter for extra effect.

Next, they went to
the paper shop and
bought a bottle of
green ink. Then they
went to the chemist
and bought

a green
sponge – exactly
like the green
sponge in the
bathroom
at home.

They already had
green towels, so
now everything
in the bathroom
would be green.

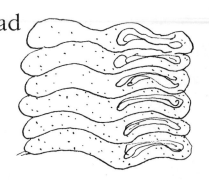

Finally, they went home and sneaked the green ink and the green sponge up into their bedroom, and put the carton of yogurt in the fridge.

Then they were ready to put the plan into action.

CHAPTER FIVE

"We had a wonderful lesson at school today," they fibbed when they sat down to supper.

"Was it about ecology, dears?" asked Mrs Norm.

"It was more about the *dangers* of too much ecology," said Mary.

"Dangers?" asked Dad, with a panicky look in his eyes. "What kind of dangers?"

"Well, sometimes parents who practise too much ecology can actually turn green," said Mary.

"Yes," said Ben. "And it's very dangerous. If you do turn green, you have to have all your skin peeled off."

Just like a banana.

Rubbish.

Rubbish.

But Mum and Dad weren't quite sure whether it was rubbish or not. Their voices sounded a bit squeaky.

Can you imagine Mr and Mrs Norm with their skin peeled off?

No wonder they were worried!

CHAPTER SIX

Getting Mum and Dad *worried*
about turning green and having to
be peeled was only the first part of
Mary's fantastic plan. The second
part was actually getting their skin
to *turn* green. She'd worked that out
as well. That's why they'd bought
the green ink and the sponge.

That night, after their bath, they only pretended to go to bed. Instead, they sneaked back into the bathroom. Mary had the green ink. Ben had the new green sponge.

They poured the green ink on to the new sponge, then went back to bed, taking the old green sponge Mr and Mrs Norm usually used with them.

Thank goodness for candlelight, they thought. It suited their plan. The house was so gloomy, you couldn't see anything properly.

After a while they heard Dad splashing about in the bath. Then he dried himself on one of the green towels. Then he went to bed. Then Mum did the same.

As soon as Mary and Ben heard Dad snoring and Mum bashing him on the nose to stop him, they sneaked back into the bathroom and, very carefully so they wouldn't get any ink over themselves, cleaned the bath.

They put the old green sponge
back where it should be and
popped the inky sponge into a
plastic bag to throw away later.
Now no one could have guessed
what had made the bath water
turn green.

In the morning, they were woken by horrible screams. Mum and Dad had discovered they'd turned green. They had absolutely no idea that the green ink had caused it.

Not only was their skin green,
but the whites of their eyes and
their tongues were as well. They
looked like two gigantic cabbages.

"Miss Jones says sometimes you
can reverse the process by eating
yak yogurt," said Mary.

"Just like the stuff that's in the
fridge," said Ben.

Mr and Mrs Norm dashed to the fridge. They grabbed the yogurt and gobbled it up wildly, their teeth crunching and grating on the bits of garden grit and cat litter Ben and Mary had poured into it the day before. It was a horrible sound.

Then there was an even more
horrible sound. It was the kind of
horrible sound someone makes
when they get grit and cat litter
caught in a hole in their tooth. Dad
roared like a demented bull and
leapt around the table clutching his
mouth. He'd lost a big filling.

Mary and Ben said he'd have to go to the dentist. But not just any old dentist. He'd have to go to a dentist who practised Natural Dentistry. Natural Dentists were specially for ecologists, they explained.

"First they scrape your teeth with pebbles. Then they saw through them with a hacksaw," said Mary.

"That's only after they've sanded them down and drilled them with a hand-drill," said Ben.

"It's all very natural," said Mary. "You'll love it."

Ben and Mary were making all
this up of course, but Dad didn't
know. The fear of having to have
his skin peeled off *and* having his
teeth sawn with a hacksaw was too
much for him.

He said he refused to have
Natural Dentistry. What's more, he
wasn't going to let anyone peel Mrs
Norm's skin off either. He said he
liked her skin where it was. On
Mrs Norm.

"I'm going back to being normal," he said.

Mrs Norm agreed. She said she wasn't going to wear stupid sacks any more. She marched upstairs and fluffed up the duvets and threw out the itchy straw blankets.

In time, the green ink wore off. Mum went back to wearing her fishnet body stocking and the red feather boa.

Dad's tooth stopped aching. He started wearing his shell-suit again and devouring vast quantities of his favourite beefburgers.

Mary's fantastic plan had worked! Mum and Dad were their normal impossible selves again!

But Mary and Ben kept the rest
of the green ink, just in case.

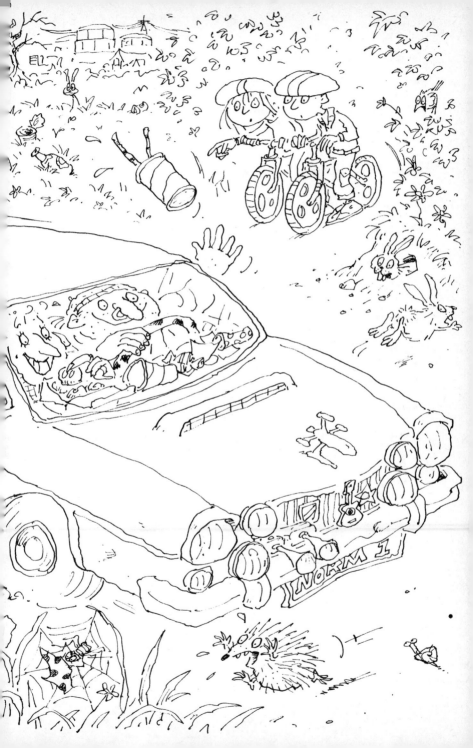

More *SPRINTERS* for you to enjoy!

- *Little Stupendo Flies High* Jon Blake   0-7445-5970-7
- *Captain Abdul's Pirate School* Colin McNaughton 0-7445-5242-7
- *The Ghost in Annie's Room* Philippa Pearce   0-7445-5993-6
- *Molly and the Beanstalk* Pippa Goodhart   0-7445-5981-2
- *Taking the Cat's Way Home* Jan Mark   0-7445-8268-7
- *The Finger-eater* Dick King-Smith   0-7445-8269-5
- *Care of Henry* Anne Fine   0-7445-8270-9
- *The Impossible Parents Go Green* Brian Patten   0-7445-7881-7
- *Flora's Fantastic Revenge* Nick Warburton   0-7445-7898-1
- *Jolly Roger* Colin McNaughton   0-7445-8293-8
- *The Haunting of Pip Parker* Anne Fine   0-7445-8294-6
- *Tarquin the Wonder Horse* June Crebbin   0-7445-7882-5

All at £3.99